.cum

Catrina Brown

GREEN IVY
PUBLISHING

Green Ivy Publishing
1 Lincoln Centre
18W140 Butterfield Road
Suite 1500
Oakbrook Terrace IL 60181-4843
www.greenivybooks.com

.cum/Catrina Brown
ISBN: 978-1-946775-71-9
Ebook: 978-1-946775-72-6

Acknowledgments

This is overwhelming . . . I am so grateful to share my world, and for people to actually read about it, I am so outdone. First, giving honor to God when I lost my faith knowing that you always had my back, and I knew better but I am grounded once again and back on track all because of you. Thank you, Lord, for my blessing. My three soldiers, Justin, Alonzo, and Russell Jr., thank you for sharing your mom with the world and giving me your support on all levels; love you all truly. To my granddaughter Jade Amena my new love. To my grandmother Laura Brown, my daughter Jade Alexis Wallace, my brother Istosh Wilson, and a host of family and friends all resting in heaven, smiling down on me. If I could have anything in the world, it would be to breathe life back into you all for you to be here, sharing this special moment with me. To my mom Gwendolyn and younger brother Tyas, thank you for providing the help that make me a better me. To my co-workers, 7–3 and 3–11 shift, thank you for being supportive, nosey (lol), and encouraging. To all my family, friends, and the supporters who has given me the strength and encouragement to tell my story.

Blessings! If I didn't mention you at this time, I will catch you in book no. 2 already in the works.

Thank you.
Sincerely,
Catrina D. Brown

Introduction

In my opinion, the creators of the online dating sites are the pimps. These sites are the platforms of the modern-day prostitution, but it's legal! A high percentage of the people, male and female, are not looking for love. They have more concerns and different agendas, seeking money for sex or material items to benefit their personal gain in order to survive. The creators get their money off the top; you do have the opportunity to join for free. Not so fast! There is always a catch to view the messages or flirts, and you have to pay the price. In addition, if you are not mindful of your money, they will renew your activation fee automatically without your knowledge, especially if you are a first-timer.

In conclusion, people showcase their goods to the highest bidder; once they find a buyer, it's showtime. For a less fraudulent legit (real) person like myself, really searching for a companion. It can be very discouraging because you have to announce to some that you are not for sale! I would love to meet that special someone to deactivate me from the sites, so for the moment, please sit back, keep an open mind, and enjoy the story of my life into the world of online dating.

Conclusion

My current situation is S-I-N-G-L-E! Awww, it's okay. I'm at peace and in a good place with myself. I have met and enjoyed the company of some nice, respectful, complicated, and few promising men. My issue is not meeting men; it is keeping a man. I can admit I have some jacked-up ways, especially when alcohol is involved, and I am working on me as we speak. I have even taken time out to apologize to some that I may have hurt because of my behavior, not realizing they may have been the "one." Some I pushed away because of the way I acted to make them not want to pursue me because of my attitude. The dating-site experience overall was entertaining, knowledgeable, and exciting. I would advise people to join for the right reasons. I will say to use common sense because there are some people that do not have your best interest at heart. Surprisingly, there are men that have never been married that are ready and really want a serious relationship or even marriage. Ladies, there is hope to find that special someone; it's a matter of patience and prayer—the Lord will lead you to the man you deserve. *Ding, ding, ding*—notification, you have new messages. Here I go again?

My Journey Looking for Mr. Goodbar

For the last two years, I've been living in the suburb of Candyland with my sons, minding my own business on my Milky Way. In the past four years, I've met men that were looking for a Payday or were Airheads, Nerds, Lemonheads, Jolly Joes, Alexander the Grape, Mike and Ike, 3 Musketeers, Charleston Chew, Twix, M&M's, Swedish Fish, Butterfinger, Chick-O-Stick, Baby Ruth, Jolly Rancher, Junior Mints, Gummy Bear, Sour Patch Kid, Hershey's, Almond Joy, York, even Whachamacallit but still no Charm Pop. So Now and Later, my thoughts of my dream man would make me Snicker, because I knew he would be Red Hot, a Whopper, and a Mound of Laffy Taffy especially with his Jawbreaker smile. I would shower him with my love of Reese's Pieces and Kisses on his Blow Pop till he Starburst in my KitKat. In parting, I know all these Skittles, Twizzlers, Kitts, Red Vines, Sour Cherries are haters and does not want me to live happily ever after, but in the end, I know I will end up with the top prize—MY REESE'S CUP.

Chapter 1

Year 2012. I was a *virgin*—that is, to online dating scene. I was separated from my so-called ex-husband, the lousy, cheating, thieving-ass son of a biscuit eater. But that's a whole other book; maybe that will be my next bestseller (wink!). Here's a little background. I have worked in law enforcement over twenty years so getting or meeting men are not an issue. It depends on what you like; there are the married ones, two-timing ones, the ones that think I'm all that because I got a job and can carry a gun, or the whatever way the wind blows I'm down. I am a beautiful, African American woman, mother of three, grandmother of one, financially and mentally stable on a good day, if you don't rub me the wrong way, good-hearted person. I don't frequent clubs, lounges, or just out in the streets to meet men on a daily basis. One evening, I was home watching TV and saw an online dating site advertisement: "African Singles Meet." I called my two sons in my room and tell them, "I'm going on this site to find me a man." They both looked at me like I was crazy and walked back out of my room, shaking their heads.

Chapter 2

One thing about me, I am not a serial dater. If someone catches my interest, I would give them my time and focus on establishing a relationship. I am a "*real*" person with a "*real*" heart, and I am open to dating. I can honestly say I would love to experience true love in my lifetime. Someone I can't live without, someone I can't wait to get home to every night, or just someone I want to share my world with and my family and be "*happy.*" My intentions were and are to physically meet someone in person, and if I feel the person is sincere, the possibility of a second date is high. I don't have time to waste, and I wouldn't want to waste anyone else's, plus some people are serious with their feelings and will hurt your ass. With the Lord's blessings, no physical harm has come to me and I know a lot of people will say her ass is crazy to meet these guys, especially in other states. My family is skeptical and concerned for my safety when I go out on dates to meet the guys I met online. I would pray on the situation because you never know if he is the person he's claiming to be, a pyscho, a murderer, or even a rapist.

Chapter 3

I am woman, and can admit, I don't make good choices. Honestly, I don't lol my past husbands—yeah you heard me H-U-S-B-A-N-D-S, plural, meaning three were something else. One of my issues is finding a good man, not to say they were not just not for me. I always feel I could save the world always wearing my cape, seeing the good and potential in people that actually was never there but a mirage. But I still didn't give up on love. My first marriage, 1989–1990, was abusive, unhealthy, and drug use on both parts, just a jacked-up combination. We stayed in a basement apartment and used to fight so much. I used to hide weapons (screwdrivers, knives, and/or anything that could help me get this nigger up off my ass). We married for the sake of our son but knew we shouldn't have a week prior to our wedding; we had a fight out of this world but went through with it because the invitations were already sent out. This union only lasted two years. My blessing, my numero uno son Justin, was born and that is one thing I would never regret from this marriage. In 1995, I fell in love with a stripper husband no. 2; why I called him that because he worked that thang like never before—lol. This marriage was abusive; he cheated and just flat out didn't give a fuck. I almost killed him accidentally after one of our fights. I stabbed him in his chest later on, finding out it was one inch from his lungs. God saved me that day. One of my blessings from this union was my beautiful baby girl, Jade Alexis; I was so happy I had my son Justin Avery and now my baby girl. I was scheduling my tubal ligation but my co-worker Darlene, who, over the years, became one of my best friends to this date, told me not to have the procedure because it was permanent and you never know you may want more children down the line.

Chapter 4

I pondered the idea and listened to her and didn't go through with the procedure. I was working the midnight shift a day after April Fools' Day and my kids had went over to their grandmother's house the prior evening with my husband to help his mother move. He called and said they were going to spend the night and will be home in the morning. I got off work that morning, went home, cleaned the house, and cooked dinner, waiting for their arrival. Instead, I received a phone call from his sister and a detective asking me to come to the police station. I asked him if my babies were all right; he said yes, then I asked, "What did my husband do?"

He put my husband on the phone. He stated, "Everything is okay, meet me at my mother's house." I asked my cousin Owedia to ride with me; something is wrong and she said, "Just calm down and let's go see what is going on." I was driving from the east side of Chicago to the west side hysterical, not understanding what could have happened. I pulled up in front of his mom's building for this time of morning at 8:30 AM; it was strange because there were a lot of people out in the projects. I exited my car and walked toward the building; there was a crowd of people at the first floor apartment at a neighborhood favorite home whom everybody loved. My husband stepped out of the crowd and stated, "Jade is gone." I could not, to this day, wish that on my worst enemy.

Chapter 5

DEVASTED. He said, "It was an accident and my son laid on her while she sleeping." UNBELIEVABLE! Not once in my soul or in my heart did I believe that was true. The story his family explained to me was that Jade's aunts, who were teenagers at the time, were babysitting because her father left for the night to be with one of his hoes. That my son climbed off the top the top bunk of the bunk beds they all were sleeping in to use the restroom, but instead of climbing back up top, he crossed over the eldest of the trio and laid on my baby. BULLSHIT! Both families were very hurt, upset, and divided; the funeral service was just as separated my family was pissed because they lied on my five-year-old son. We went through counseling with my son and myself but could never put the pieces together on what really happened that night. I got pregnant intentionally soon after because I wanted my baby back. But that was not what the Lord had for me; instead, he blessed me son no. 2, my chocolate drop Alonzo. After all I endured, I found out my husband's mistress, the one he was with the night my daughter died and at my daughter's funeral had given birth to her daughter five months after my son was born. Heartbroken and to add insult to my misery, she named her daughter after my daughter's middle name and had a second child, a son, the following year and named him after the same middle name my husband and son shared. I told her, "If I ever catch you . . . your ass is mine."

To this present day, I never met her. We were at my son's grandmother's house so I can pick up my son. This woman left immediately. I asked, "Who was that?" Everyone was silent until my son told me that was her. That girl tore ass getting out that house—lmao. That is the past; I can't bring my baby back, and I am at peace with them all.

Chapter 6

That marriage ended fast as it began, 1995–1998. The best event that came from this was my experience and giving birth to my angel, Jade Alexis Wallace (December 2, 1994 to April 2, 1995) and son Alonzo. See you soon, my love. In 1998, I purchased my first new home for me and my sons in the Cottage Grove Heights neighborhood. I was thirty years old and excited and finally happy. Time had passed. I took a break from men and practiced celibacy and learned to love me for me. In this timeframe, I met some very special people whom I shared some great times with. One I want to mention is Pearl, who lost her life on June 11, 2016. Rest in heaven and watch over my Jade. Love you always.

Chapter 7

In 2002, I met a nice young man while going to see my aunt sing at a popular blues club on the north side of Chicago. We hit it off instantly. I learned he was sweet and a real stand-up guy, nothing I ever experienced in my marriages. He would spend the weekends with me, give me money to purchase everything I needed for a memorable time with him, and even a diamond, baguette, heart-shaped ring. I felt I died and went to heaven. We dated strong for three months and my world came crashing down. He came to my home one afternoon and said, "Trina I love my kids." I had a confused look on my face. He continued and said if we continued, he couldn't see them. He confessed he was married and his wife and son lived in Germany. I was in awe. I never knew he was married I was hurt and felt I couldn't win from losing. I will never forget Mr. R. even though he betrayed me. We were still great friends till his recent untimely death I will always have love for him—woe is me. On my way home from work one afternoon driving on the Dan Ryan Expressway, I met husband no. 3, where I should have left his ass. If I knew prior to getting involved with him what I know now, I would have sped off—damn, damn, damn! We spotted each other and began visually flirting and decided to pull over. Our conversation was good and we started dating soon after. I looked up weeks later, this nigger was moving in. We dated for a year and planned this huge wedding out of nowhere. Mr. R. pops up at my family church and tells my mom he needs to talk to me ASAP. We make arrangements and met for drinks, and he drops the bomb.

Chapter 8

r. R. stated, "I'm divorced and I am ready for us."

I'm looking like a deer caught in headlights and I said, "I'm engaged, and I planned the wedding. Money has been spent. I can't do that."

He said, "I asked you to wait for me, let me take care of this, and to be patient." He then said, "I will reimburse all the money that was spent, and I want to spend the rest of my life with you and the boys, and I never stopped loving you."

This fucked my whole world up. I had feelings for my husband to be, but my love ran deep for Mr. R. I made the choice to marry my fiancée, a decision I always regret that I chose the wrong man—the lying, cheating, and stealing this man put me and my family through no one was safe. I'm still kicking my own ass with both feet; this marriage lasted longer than the others because I didn't want another failed marriage under my belt. I was not an angel. I did my dirt and cheated as well, but the strange thing is, I wanted to get caught so he could feel some of the pain he caused me. My joy out of five years of misery, the five years of some happiness was my baby boy RJ. We divorced in 2012, I had two, not one divorce parties—the pre and finale, because of my newfound freedom. This divorce was one of the happiest moments of my life. Now you have been updated through some of my trials and tribulations on how I came to the decision to engage in the world of online dating. Buckle up, sit back, and enjoy the ride.

Chapter 9

How hard could this be? I am a real person looking for love, so I filled out the questionnaire and put my picture on my profile and instantly received flirts. I began viewing the pictures, and I was impressed; some of the men on the site were handsome. I thought I hit the jackpot. I began receiving messages and flirts from men all over the United States. My first encounter was from a man named Fred from Texas; he was fine-ass hell, well-built, light-skinned, made you want smack your momma. His profile stated he was in the army and ready to settle down. We began chatting back and forth on the site. He told me he was stationed in Iraq and his tour would be over in two months and asked if we could meet at the airport on his way back to Texas. Our only way of communicating was through Yahoo Messenger due to him being in Iraq; he couldn't call on the phone. This went on daily for a month. Here comes the bull; he sends me a message saying he was moving to another area and didn't own the laptop he was using to message me from and if I could buy him one because his credit cards were tied up due to him being overseas. I responded, "Awwwwwwwww, hell nawwww-www," and that was the end of Fred fine ass a year or so later, his slick ass was back on the site using another name and different profile.

Then I started talking to Sebaston from the site from Indianapolis; he said he worked demolition on the highway. He was 6'3" and 240 pounds. Enough said. We talked on the phone a for few weeks; everything was good. He even invited me to an expo, a popular event held in Indianapolis every year. Until this monkey had the nerve to ask me, "Can you help me get my motorcycle out the shop?"

I looked at the phone as if I was getting punked. I was waiting for Ashton Kutcher to come out my closet. *Click*. My phone died. My fault. LOL.

Next, it was Tyrone from Chicago. Bless his heart, we talked and met in person at the lakefront. We had a good conversation, but I knew it wouldn't amount to anything. Physically, he wasn't my type, but he was nice and respectful; he still hasn't given up on me to the present time.

Chapter 10

Jermaine came out of nowhere from Kalamazoo, MI. he was six feet, muscular, and chocolate. We connected mentally, and I was on the road like Madea down 94. I made it to his home in two hours and some change. He looked better in person than his pictures, and my insides was screaming. He cooked me dinner and had the wine chilling. I was impressed. He was a truck driver, had his own, and wanted something out of life. We talked and laughed the night away. He made me feel so comfortable as if I've known him for a lifetime. I told him it was time for me to go; it was getting late. He said, "It's too late for you to be driving. I will give you something to sleep in, no strings attached, and you can have my bedroom for the night."

He was the perfect gentlemen. We slept the night away and parted that morning with a simple kiss on the cheek—until next time. His birthday was in the following weeks. He had a family gathering. I met his sisters and friends. We had a great time and we played cards, had cocktails, danced, and partied the night away. He passed out drunk.

I helped him to his room, put him to bed, cleaned up, and got ready for bed. As he was lying there, knocked out snoring, my horny ass was rubbing on him and kissing his earlobes. This man's dick was so big, thick, and long, I was drooling. He was out of it, so I rolled over, went to sleep, pouting like the spoiled brat that I am because I wanted him so bad. Morning came and he was still hungover, and I was still horny. He showed some signs of life and that was my cue. I straddled and rode his horse dick like I was in the Kentucky Derby. After our session, I got up, showered, got dressed, and kissed him good-bye—till the next episode . Our next months of our relationship looked promising, even discussing with him about moving closer so I wouldn't have to travel as far to see him. But I knew that our last physical encounter maybe our last because of a previous conversation we had; he asked me to join him and a female friend in a threesome. I explained to him I've never had a threesome and never desired one. I am selfish and don't like sharing. He kept pushing the issue, so it was bye-bye, Kalamazoo. I took a break for a couple of months to gather my thoughts, but the site was like crack cocaine! *Ding! Ding!* Crack!

Chapter 11

So I eased my crazy ass back on there just a glutton for punishment. I talked to a few more guys. One was Otis, but we didn't meet physically. Sometimes it's best to be friends or acquaintances rather than date. My hair is platinum blond, so I stick out in a crowd, and I may add, it looks great on me. One afternoon, I was getting my car serviced at the Dodge dealership on Western. I was standing outside, talking on my phone and the other line beeped; it was Andre. We talked on the phone on and off for months but never planned a date; we just enjoyed talking to each other from time to time.

He said, "I just saw someone that looks like you. Are you on Western?"

I said, "That is me, and why didn't you pull over?" which I thought it was the strangest thing. He said, "I have a meeting to attend, but I will call you later to see if we can meet." I was spooked because the realization of being on the site is, people can see you and you don't have to know them at all. You are open to the public for the world to see you. I got paranoid. My next plan of action was to get off the radar. My next beauty shop appointment, I dyed my hair cinnamon bronze. I had to go in hiding. I was hot on the streets. LMAO!

Chapter 12

Mr. Terrance was forty-ish, bald, chocolate, and athletic-build (basketball player figure), definitely my speed. We chitchatted; he was cool. He said he worked at Ford, owned his own home, took care of his of mother, went to church regularly, has five brothers and two adult kids. We hit it off, but he was showboat and wanted eye candy on his arm, someone he can showcase like he was King Dingaling. We met for drinks at a local lounge, a place a lot of my co-workers frequented, so it wasn't a place for me. I walked in and he was sitting at a table with his male friends; they were looking at me like I was fresh meat. I told him I will at the bar; he politely excused himself and followed me. We talked and had a few drinks. I had to give to him. He was very attentive and a perfect gentleman; he had to be because he has sisters. I was looking cute, outfit was tight, and my sexy walk had the boys in the yard going he was really feeling like he was the man, but the feeling was mutual. He wasn't alone. It was getting late; we both had to work in the morning. He walked me to my car, and we parted ways with a nice hug and wonderful feelings about our first encounter. Our second date was at the same damn lounge—smh . . . I asked him, "Can you go outside the neighborhood past the viaduct?" He just smiled, but in my mind, I was saying, "You got me twice. You not going to get me again." We made an attractive couple but this lounge outing every week with his buddies was his life, and I explained to him I like going to other places that serve other than hot wings and extra strong gasoline long islands. He said, "Okay, next time."

So you know what that meant, there was no next time because this was the only place he wanted to go.

Chapter 13

Now, it's Jermaine; other than the site, we connected in more ways than one he was from my rivalry old high school, but he graduated a few years before me, but he was my real rivalry. He took the winning of the wagon wheel to heart. It was a tradition between the two schools that whichever team won got to keep the wagon and the bragging rights. He would make comments like he wasn't sure if he should be talking to me because I was the enemy because I went to the other school. I would be listening to this old fool like, "Are you serious?" and believe me, he was. We both had been out of high school for over twenty-five years. He was a decent guy; besides that, just relocating back to Chicago, he was a single father and starting over. He was a survivor and a go-getter. He was transitioning when we started talking, staying in hotels or with friends until he found steady work to provide for him and his daughter. I give credit where it was due. He had a great personality and speaking voice, which made him excel as a car salesmen, but he was just stuck back in the memories of high school. I removed myself from the equation so he can continue to grow and be all he could for whoever it was; it just wasn't me. We are good friends to this day—no love lost.

Chapter 14

My profile stalkers: co-workers that I meet online only. They will view my profile daily, knowing that the person on the profile is actually me and see me and won't say a word. I even approached someone and introduced myself, and we were in class together a week. He did not say one word to me all week, but that last day, he had the nerve to go back on my page; that is crazzzzzzyyy. I have walked in the building with some of them. Crickets. In my opinion, the dating site is not anything to be embarrassed about; it's just a different way to go about dating. One guy, Tom, since the beginning, when I first got on the site has always left me messages or shown interest. So I finally responded to his message; we chatted back and forth, and he left me his number. I called him and got no answer. Later that evening, he left me a message stating he thought he saw me at a gas station but didn't say anything because he didn't want to appear creepy. I told him what was creepy was to come back on my page and say you've seen me but didn't say anything to me in person. I must admit, it does make you paranoid if someone is staring/looking at you because you don't know if they know you from the site or work. I have worked around some bad elements on a daily basis for over twenty years.

Chapter 15

I was no stranger to New York. I used to organize bus trips two to three times a year for shopping excursions. So when eventually after months of talking to my Jersey boo, Rashan, I was comfortable meeting him in Manhattan because I was familiar with the area. When we first started off talking, I wasn't interested because of the distance, but he wouldn't back down; he was very persistent. I loved his accent. Talking on the phone went from once a day to over seven to eight times a day. Our connection was natural, our conversations flowed, and we always had something new or interesting to talk about every time. This one particular day, he called on my off day and our conversation was so deep and meaningful I gave in and gave him my all. He was handsome, with dimples, and with a heart of gold. Around Valentine's Day, he asked me for my address. At first I was hesitant. The following week, I received a beautiful card with cash. I was shocked because we haven't met in person but Skyped and talked on a daily basis. I told him, "I'm coming to meet you."

We decided on New York instead of Jersey because I knew how to get around so if it didn't work out, I could still enjoy myself. I bought my plane ticket, booked my room at my usual hotel I frequented whenever I visited, plus I knew Broadway like it was Stoney Island. I was nervous as hell because in a month's span, I had grown feelings for this man, even felt I loved him. The day we met face-to-face, we approached each other in the middle of the sidewalk, kissing like we were invisible. We tongued kiss over and over it felt like forever. We separated, smiling like school kids and checked in our room; he was everything I expected. The plan was for him to come back to Chicago with me; at this point, we both fell head over heels in love. We got in the room. As I hugged him, I could feel his big dick on my stomach. My pussy was so wet it was dripping juices down my thighs. He said, "Wait I got a birthday gift for you." He gave me a Kindle tablet. I was so excited because I've been wanting one for a while.

Chapter 16

He then got down one knee and proposed to me with the most beautiful two-carat diamond engagement ring. I was blown away. I hugged him so tight and gave him the deepest, juiciest, best tongue kiss he ever got in his life. I felt his thickness rubbing and grinding against my pussy. I damn near came johnny on the spot. I heard the horns from heaven playing and my mind screaming, "Thank you, Jesus. I finally met someone who's attractive, genuine, loving, and loving him some me." He got undressed. My eyes watered, and I had to catch myself from drooling. I saw him nude on Skype via computer, but it was nothing like having the real thing, baby. He sucked my pussy so good I came over and over and over; his dick was the bomb! This man had skills with his tongue, his lips, his touch, and he knew how to work my pussy into a lather. We were a perfect fit—not too much, not too big, just right—especially being celibate, it was painful, but it was pure pleasure. We eventually got out the room for some air and enjoyed the New York nightlife. We had a ball; we ate, drank, and celebrated our engagement, my birthday, and our new love for each other. He kept his word and gave me $500 for the hotel room and treated me like the queen I was; his word in my book was gold. He came to Chicago with me where the party still continued; I was on cloud nine.

Chapter 17

The following weeks, I was rushing home from work, getting fucked royally in more ways than one every day. He had a dick that wouldn't quit. I called it bounce back; he could cum and his dick was rock hard instantly and ready for the next round. It was so good I threw away my vibrator—LOL. For the next four months I was Rashan's heaven. He found a job and transitioning from New Jersey to Chicago went quite well. My world was turned upside down with the snap of a finger; I had been at the happiest point of my entire adult life. Prior to meeting me, he had unresolved child support issues, court issues, and his mother became ill, so he had to return to Jersey to resolve his unfinished business. We would visit each other three to five months for four or five days, and it was priceless—each visit better than the last. I loved going to New York and Jersey and enjoyed him to the fullest when he came to Chicago; we had a whirlwind romance. This back-and-forth engagement went on for over two years. I was content with spending time with him sparingly, plus I had my personal space. I never got tired of him because

I truly loved him, and when he would come to town, his clothes were in the closet, personal possessions intact, and his heart was at his home, waiting on him. The reality of our fairytale was I wasn't ready for marriage, and at age forty-seven, I didn't want to start over. By that, I mean he had to learn his way around Chicago, get a car, and he was still paying child support, and I couldn't see myself winning and I was tired of losing.

Chapter 18

The arguments became more frequent and his selfish head emerged, and the real Rashan stood up and thank God before I moved this motherfucker into my home. I still have love for him and no regrets, but I will be honest, I miss his ass to death, especially that big dick smh . . . After licking my wounds and realizing my Jersey boo was not my Mr. Right but instead Mr. Dead Wrong, we still communicate and express our love for each other, and he still claims he's going to be my husband. Eventually, I tootsie-rolled ass back online in the dating pool.

I met Zach, a forklift driver for Avon over eighteen years, was very nice, respectful, and established. He had one adult child, owned his own home, car, and was easy on the eyes. Our first meeting after talking on the phone for a couple of weeks was spooky; he said to me, "In two months, remind me to tell you something." That threw me for a loop, but I hung in there because my nosey ass wanted to know what he had to tell me. We dated for months; he was a pleaser, and everything I wanted he would do it because he liked me a lot and that made me like him more. My happiness was very important to him. Our sex life was okay; by him being older, he had an erection issue and even bought Viagra to please me, besides the toys we added for my pleasure. He wined and dined me to no end, but the dress code was stuck back in the seventies. One time, we went to the movies; I met him at the ticket booth. He walked up in some Tommy Hilfiger carpenter bell bottoms covering his whole damn shoes. LOL. OMG, I was so embarrassed. I walked in the theater praying no one I know seen me. Who happens to be seating behind me were my co-worker and his wife. I could have melted in my chair. After the movie was over, I was stalling so they could walk out first so they wouldn't see his bell bottoms swinging in the wind. We went to the Horseshoe Casino for dinner in Binion's Steakhouse. I was impressed, but we had to walk through the whole damn casino past everybody, and he had on these damn carpenter pants. Needless to say, I saw no one and our dinner was great. We shared Christmas together, exchanged gifts, and he wanted to meet my kids and even said if he knew I would marry him; he would buy me a ring in an instant. The news he had for me after the two months of us dating was when he first laid eyes on me, he knew he wanted to spend the rest of his life with me. Our schedules collided; I was working a lot of overtime due to me buying my second home, and we faded apart. His feelings were stronger for me than mine were for his. Plus, my true feelings were still with my Jersey boo; I couldn't shake him.

Chapter 19

In November, I was hot on the online streets once again; some of the men I remembered and was still online looking for love, herpes, or something with no name. But there were new faces, so there was hope. First there was Antonio from Sauk Village, six-foot-five, and a construction worker. We began talking; he was nice, creative, and respectful, and he would recite poetry to me every day that he claimed he wrote just for me. Bullshit. We talked about three weeks and no problems, then the calls suddenly stopped, and I didn't hear from him. A month past, a few days before Christmas, and he sends a picture of himself.

I replied, "You must have sent this by accident and sent it to the wrong person."

He responded, "Catrina, how are you?"

Then I knew it was intended for me. We began talking on the phone again casually; he said the reason he stopped calling was because he was falling too fast but he couldn't stay away. I knew it was bull but entertained his nonsense.

About the fifth day after we started talking, I received a text from his phone read as follows: "This is Antonio's wife. Can you please stop sending pictures to my husband's phone?" I'm sorry he ain't shit. I am in the hospital right now with my sister who is dying. I was so outdone and mad but felt the lady's pain. I've been cheated on before. I texted her back and apologized and told her I didn't know he was married and I met him on a dating site and "I will honor your request and you and your family our in my prayers."

She texted me back and asked which site he was on and what name should she look for. My response was, "I don't want to feed into that, and again, I pray for you and your family." That was fucked up. I heard nothing more from him or his wife until recently the bastard has the nerve to be back online with the same profile and still sending me flirts. Do me a favor, Antonio. Go play in traffic, as my mother would say; it's just shameful.

Chapter 20

Mickey was on deck; he was an only child with no kids and lost both his parents years apart. He was a truck driver for over fifteen years; he was kind of shy, especially on the phone. I didn't think nothing much of it. Until his words from texting didn't match his phone conversation so my spidey sense went off. We talked a few weeks, plus I was going to Washington, DC, so our in person meeting would have to be put off for a few weeks. We exchanged pictures and texted while I was on vacation and decided to meet for cocktails once I came back home. While away, he sent me a photo of himself and it looked as if he had breast. I was like, hold up, wait a minute! I texted him and said, "At the angle of the picture, it looks like you have breast. LOL."

His reply was shocking because he didn't get offended and kind of played it off. I was returning home that Tuesday. We had a date set, and he suddenly changed it after I sent the breast comment. He stated he has a scheduled surgery for that day for a pre-existing slip disc condition that came out of nowhere. I said, "Would you like for me to come visit you in the hospital?"

He said no; he had to do this alone. I backed off and my famous words came into play: "Take care and be blessed." In June, this sorry sap sucker texted me, saying he was still in rehab for his back and hasn't forgotten me. My theory was, I've been fuckin' catfished by a goddamn girl, ain't this a bitch.

Chapter 21

I had a couple of more locals. We chitchatted, but nothing came of it. There was Marvel, a single father from the west side, and Roy, a southeast native. I wasn't attracted to Roy, but he had beautiful hazel eyes, and Marvel, we connected a little but he turned out to be a liar. I wasn't surprised.

Sal from Michigan, we met and connected instantly and made our first date weeks later and met at the Michigan outlet mall. I was attracted to Sal; he was 6'3", solid 230 pounds, handsome, dressed nice, smelled good, and chocolate, all wrapped up in one. We had dinner; he was cool. Our conversation flowed, and our evening didn't feel forced, just natural. We continued talking weeks and months on end and even planned an out-of-town excursion to New Orleans. Our second date was at the Blue Chip Casino spa and hotel where we were staying for the night. I really liked him. I made us a conversation plate of grapes, cheese, and strawberries and you know I really liked him. I made a banana pudding from scratch and gave him a

belated Christmas gift. I got there first and set up everything and he came shortly after with champagne, a red
gift box, and a fine-ass piece of a man. We exchanged gifts
and both were pleased; he was impressed and grateful that
I took time out to prepare for our special date. We went
downstairs to gamble and eat dinner then returned to the
room for dessert.

Chapter 22

He set up his iPod, played some music, filled our glasses, and wooed me with his tantalizing conversation. We talked, laughed, and popped open a second bottle of champagne—now the fun begins. We kissed, sucked, and seductively licked each other tongues, rubbing and touching in both our intimate spots, breathing in between our breaks for air. Bottle number 3, he was playing dangerously. Catrina left, and after the second bottle, Trixie came in and nobody is safe when she comes out. I straddled him and grinded on his dick until I bust a nut all on his hard dick. I got up and licked and sucked his dick so good like the pro I was after the foreplay and the quick fuck I just received; everything went blank. I woke up the next morning with a snoring bull and confused, not knowing if I got fucked for real or not. We parted ways with him promising me a round two and the fuck of a lifetime with less champagne. Sal and I continued to keep in touch months afterward and expressing our love but not physically connecting due to the weather conditions; we just met in the wrong season. I had gotten to a point with him that I was not going to allow my feelings to be hurt again, but he wouldn't let me go and kept trying to pull me back into his life. Just say, I'm a glutton for punishment; recently, I went to his home to rekindle our everlasting flame. Our chemistry and love was there as if no time has passed, and I will always cherish that about us. The next two bottles of champagne, Trixie did her thing, and the snoring bull lost the race once again. Deuces. He still says to this day he is the one for me and he loves me to death and will continue to show his love. I will admit I have love for him but I don't have time for the games so I quit you win.

Chapter 23

I had connected with a few out-of-town boos—Jerry from Philly, Bob from Indianapolis, Ken from New York, and Larry from New Orleans. Some I still talk to this present date, and some I don't. I was conflicted about starting another out-of-town relationship because of the distance. Don't get me wrong, I can appreciate a long-distance relationship. But I was just tired of driving over two hours for a date or flying to another state just for a dinner date. This dating process was not based on how good you kiss, how big your dick was, or even how great your head game was; it was about getting to get know someone's heart—that in itself means the world to me. Another caller was Bill from Indiana, a truck driver, age fifty-two, has kids, and lived with his brother. We met up at a bowling alley and enjoyed an afternoon of fun; he was six feet, thick, handsome, and talked a lot of shit. We parted ways, promising to keep in touch, but as time went on, the true Bill emerged. Let me go back prior to us meeting; he said he lost his brother and had to pay for the entire service. The first sign of bull was, he couldn't work because he was sick and had to be on antibiotics for ten days. Second sign, the water pump went out on his car, and third sign was his phone was cut off because he couldn't pay his bill because he wasn't working. The kicker, he had the nerve to ask me to help him pay his bill so he could continue talking to me. You know what was next, "take care and be blessed."

Chapter 24

The clouds blew in Marshawn and Tommy. I met both of them on the same day. The conversation with Marshawn was stronger. Tommy was a know-it-all, so I knew he wouldn't last long; his days were numbered. Marshawn, I met a couple of days later at Starbucks; he was nice, muscular, dark chocolate, and stable. He was fine until he smiled; his teeth were gold yellow and jacked up; he had a smile that look like a jack-o'-lantern; those two sank real quick. Then came Simon. His pics on his profile were impressive—tall, caramel, and handsome. We began talking and hit it off, and he told me he lost his adult son recently in an automobile accident. My heart was heavy because I could identify what he was going through losing a child is very painful, but his was much worse; he had his son for twenty-five years. Our conversations continued, and our bond became closer day by day. He said he was a DJ at a popular lounge on the south side of Chicago and rehabbed homes on the side. He invited me to hear him spin at his job; when I entered, he was actually the man on his profile. I was pleased. We shared a couple of cocktails and enjoyed our evening. Our second date, we had lunch at a Mexican restaurant near my home and then a movie. I was liking this guy more and more each week. I decided to let him come by my home, and my sons freaked out because I don't bring men by my house, but they were respectful; they had no choice because I pay the cost to be the boss.

Chapter 25

During the visit, he told me he rehabbed homes and could paint my house for no cost, and whatever repairs I needed, he would take care of it, that I just get the materials. I was overwhelmed; he even encouraged to have a birthday party at my house for myself and would DJ and even order food for the party. Reluctantly, I agreed to have the party, but in the back of my mind, I felt he was moving too fast or either trying to move in. Weeks before the party, all the skeletons came falling out the closet. He claimed he lived with a cousin and was looking for a place, but at age fifty-one couldn't have company. I politely told him he could not move in with me, and I didn't need anything from him as far as the party or rehabbing my home; this was our last conversation.

A month later, while at the beauty shop getting my hair done, a friend of my beautician's friend came in. We all were talking about our jobs and a young lady mentioned she barmaids at various lounges on the south side. I asked her if she knew Simon. She said, "Yes, he just got married.

Do you know his wife?"

I played it off but was not surprised because he was trying to find a new home with whomever would have taken him in. Weeks after, I was strolling on the site and this lousy, two-timing dog was on there and had the nerve to view my page. I sent him a message and told him, "I heard you got married."

His response was, "You know you didn't hear that I'm not married, and I don't plan on marrying nobody. You got the wrong one."

My next response was "Wow" and "You don't have to worry about me ever contacting you, I apologize and continued blessings."

The following month, my high school reunion was held at the place he worked, and do you know, that nigger is still mad and didn't speak and rolled his eyes. I should have gotten him a T-shirt saying "NO BITCHASSNESS." Lmao!

Chapter 26

ere comes Ronnell from Philly; he was intelligent, established, and stubborn. He had two daughters, two dogs, and a foster client who was a grown-ass man, Derrick. They paid a nice piece of change for taking in challenged and troubled people in their area. We talked and connected in such a way that in months, our courtship grew immediately. I told him, "I want to see you."

He said, "Okay, let's make arrangements." I booked my flight and a hotel and planned on meeting Mr. Right. He stated, "I got half on your room, but I got a five-bedroom home. You're free to stay here, and I will pay all our entertainment and dinners with no funny business and you can save money and spend more on shopping." I was jumping in with both feet; my only reservation is his dogs. He convinced me they were well trained and they wouldn't be near and he would put them up in an upstairs bedroom. He picked me up from the airport in my favorite car looking like Rick Ross in a cute way. I was excited, and we made our way to his home, me still dreading seeing those two big-ass dogs. They greeted us at the door; they were H-U-G-E. He talked me into coming in and actually, they weren't thinking about me, which I was shocked and felt I was more at ease. Our first night, we chilled after a day of shopping and dinner, and we made back to his house and they were on point; every move he made, they were on top-flight security. We exchanged gifts. I made him a gift box filled with chocolate-covered strawberries, pretzels, rice crispy treats, and a bedazzled mason jar with a Tupac T-shirt inside.

Chapter 27

He gave me a pair of stillettos, perfume, and a gospel CD; he was the perfect gentlemen. I overlooked his stubbornness because his positive qualities outweighed the negative ones; the thing is, with two bosses you're definitely going to have a fight. I understood him because when you're independent, you don't have to put up with anyone's nonsense. He was strong-minded, and we would clash but ended our debates with love. At bedtime, we snuggled, kissed, and held each other like there was no tomorrow, and we both gave each other that vibe, and next it was let's get it on. He lifted me up off the bed and laid me down gently in the middle of the bed and spread my thighs in V shape and licked and teased my pussy into full ecstasy. His tongue was so thick and filled my entire slit down to my asshole, licking me into full-lathered orgasm; he didn't stop until he pulled my second nut out, until I squirted into his mouth. I took all his dick in my wet box as if it would be my last; we both came together, kissing passionately, tasting my sweet pussy on his lips.

Whew, the first night was the bomb. I was so into us, I didn't realize until I went to the bathroom. The two dogs were lying next to the bed while I getting my Vanessa Del Rio on; unbelievably, he loved them damn dogs to death; they slept in his room every night. The next day, we went out for the day Derrick joined us; he was cool, and I didn't see anything abnormal with him. He acted just like the detainees I see at work five days a week. I was prepared for the worst. I was shocked Derrick was hilarious and intelligent, I might add. I pulled him to side and told him and said, "Ain't nothing wrong with you and your ass got a lot of sense." He just laughed and agreed with me.

Chapter 28

Ronnell was a gentlemen; he took me out to dinner every night, and I but had to almost fight him over my food. He would always eat some of my food or share a drink, take the very last piece of food home, even if it was a crumb. One of our connections we shared was great weight loss regimen so we could identify with each other not eating a lot. But this motherfucker constantly was eating, and he would also showboat and bragging about platinum cards, the real money he earned was from Derrick. He got nerve-wracking after day 3. I was so tempted to buy an early plane ticket home. He complained and nagged about everything and didn't know how to let things go; he complained about the way people drove, he complained about Derrick and even a piece of paper on the ground for hours. I was like, this guy is going to have heart attack. He fussed, fussed, and fussed.

One day, Derrick drunk most of the coffee that Ronell had prepared for some protein shakes. He yelled from the top of his lungs for over thirty minutes, the dogs ran and hid, and I just stood there in shock. I told him I can buy more coffee, and please don't let this ruin our day because we were on our way out to enjoy downtown Philadelphia. While we were out, he was still talking about the situation. My feelings were hurt because I really wanted us to work, but I knew with all the events even though I had a good time this would be my last visit to Philly.

Chapter 29

So my birthday was rolling around. I took a break from the line to enjoy the festivities of my birthday still alone and not giving up on love. I decided in May to jump back in the fire but took a different approach. My belief is the Lord is preparing me for the man I deserve. My failed marriages/relationships are lessons to teach me, not to make the same mistakes I made before. I began my search and met Kethan from Florida; he catches my eye on the profile. This time around, I didn't ask the men to be a certain height or weight, or they had to have a certain income, or that distance was a factor. His dimpled smile was gorgeous, he was employed, and his personality was off the charts. We talked and flirted back and forth and decided to exchange numbers; he had a southern twang in his voice, which was very nice. I told him my occupation, and he told me he had a confession; he said he did twelve years in the penitentiary for selling drugs. He said he has been out three years working as a truck driver, owned his own car, and had his own apartment. He went on to say he was ready to relocate so if I could overlook his past, will I be willing to accept him. I said my phone was dying I need to charge my phone. . . . After a few hours past he left me a voicemail on my phone saying he was depressed, and he was trying to fight his demons and he had go through this process alone. I raised my hands to the sky and said, "There is a GOD."

Chapter 30

Freako the paramedic for over nineteen years was fine, fine, fine, muscular, tall, and handsome. He was very quiet and kept to himself. I had seen him throughout my years of working there; we may or may not have spoken, but in my mind, he had my insides screaming every time I saw him. So when I saw his profile on the site, I was totally shocked; he had no kids, owned his own home, and had two cars. He had just got a promotion with a prominent city office and seeing him on the site threw me off. We spotted each other on the site and chitchatted. I told him where I worked, and he said, "I've never seen you at work."

I told him I'm seventy-five pounds lighter; he said, "That's why I don't remember you." We decided to meet for drinks and both were very pleased and had great conversation as we talked and drank the night away, promising to have a second date soon. He called a few weeks later and invited me to dinner at Chi Tung restaurant on Ninety-fifth Street. Our dinner was delicious as always, especially with this fine-ass man; in front of me it felt like Christmas. He invited me back to his home for drinks. I agreed. He had a very nice home; we sat and had a couple glasses of wine and a few pecks, lip smacking, and tongue waggling in between all the laughter and the chemistry we shared. He invited to his bedroom, stood me up, and undressed me slowly, piece by piece, kissing each section where he removed each piece of my clothing. He laid me down and licked my pussy like it was a tootsie pop, and he was to get to my creamy center. He licked me clean after I came down to the last drop. I had to repay for the bomb head he just gave me. I sucked and licked him until to point of no return; he couldn't take it no more and got on top of me and entered. He felt like he died and went to heaven. He screamed, "My baby feels so good." We fucked each other like our life depended on it to live until we both came in unison. Our date ended with smiles and promises of round 3.

Months later, it was New Year's Eve and he asked me to go a party with him, and I said yes; he said, "First, do you like girls?"

I said no. He said that's why we didn't get together again and you probably couldn't accept my lifestyle. I had the Scooby Doo look on my face: Huuuuuuuu uuuuu huuuh? I said, "You are absolutely correct." That was my exit; he still contacts me on the site every now and then. They can't get enough of Trixie. I have the utmost respect for him and his honesty; he left me a message on the site recently and told me I was beautiful, but the only thing he could offer right now is a great time and sex because he was not ready for a serious relationship. Thanks but no thanks. Peace.

Chapter 31

Next, it was Sampson. He worked at prominent hospital over seven years as a sergeant in public safety, and he also worked for Homeland Security and other law enforcement agencies in the city. He had one daughter, was a deacon of his church for over twenty years, financially stable, and established. We talked every day, and our first date was to go see Chrissette Michelle in concert; it was really nice, and we had a great time. We went for walks and spent quality time together, trying to establish a friendship or maybe a future relationship. I invited him to a family function; he came and fit in right away like he knew everyone, which I saw the potential of this going further.

There was one thing that bothered me and it was that wandering eye; he was handsome with shades on, but when he took them off, that eye started doing his own thing and this was something I had to adjust to if I wanted this man. One day, he called from his job and told me he quit, and he would talk to me later. I was stunned and wondering what could have happened because he loved that job and was like RoboCop. He was a very nice guy and respectful, and I couldn't see him beating anyone up, so my other theory had to be sexual harassment. Once we got a chance to talk, he said it was an incident with a female employee that was a lesbian, and it was over her wearing a bulletproof vest. He said he received several complaints about harassment due to the fact he has always had problems with his employees not listening or taking orders from him because he was a know-it-all. My issue with all that was his honesty; this situation occurred prior to us, so just be straight and let me know what it is, so I wouldn't be walking around blind. He didn't want to be honest and was contemplating moving out of Illinois; to me, that showed guilt. I decided to end us because of lies, and felt he wasn't being 100 percent honest with me and didn't give me the option if I wanted to deal with his situation or not. Blessings.

Chapter 32

Melvin was a divorcee real estate developer that rehabs homes, and he was a big guy and easy on the eyes. We shared one of the same friends, and he knew my brother that I lost a year and half ago. We had a bond, and he could understand and relate to my job because his best friend worked there also. We had good phone conversations and Facetime a lot with promises of meeting face-to-face because we were compatible in more ways than one. My co-worker and Melvin were tighter than tight sometimes—too tight for my comfort. I even told him one night, "I'm not going to be in competition with your friend." The one thing that was in the back of my mind, his best friend and my brother were close friends for years. His best friend had a party at his house, and my brother and him had words and he got his buddies to kick my brother out the party. I wanted to ask him, was he one of the ones that put their hands on my brother, even though my brother is no longer here, but I felt some kind of way about that, but I decided to leave well enough alone. Melvin had promised once he returned back from his trip with his best friend in Jamaica, we would get together for our date. I was like, in my mind, two men going to Jamaica, ohhhh, okay. Also the prior week, before going on the trip, which we could have met, but he spent the whole weekend partying with his best friend so that rubbed me the wrong way already. They went on the trip; he Facetimed me to show me he was thinking about me but looking at his friend across the table in his face too much. The last straw was when he returned, he said he was interested in me and was feeling some kind of way about me and needed to talk to his friend about this situation. Hold the presses. I told him, "Can't nobody tell you about me but me." So he felt his friend had the best advice to give him, so I threw in the white towel.

Chapter 33

Maury, the streets and sanitation worker for twenty-five years was six-foot-five, stocky, established, and was a nice guy. We talked a few weeks; he called daily to check up on me, which I enjoyed the attention. We met a popular lounge, had a few drinks, and I had to cut it off before Trixie clowned. We had a cool time. We continued talking for weeks, but one of our conversations, threw me for a loop. He told me he had been talking to a young man from the site that was gay. I asked him why he said he found their conversations interesting and funny. This man was over fifty, retiring from the city in five years, owned his own home and cars, and handsome. But he loved to be entertained by this gay man, which is nothing is wrong with that; just be who you are and be honest with yourself and own your shit, so that was my exit stage left.

Now I meet Buck, the sarcastic associate pastor just graduating with his BA in psychiatry. He was athletic, tall, bald, with no kids and was just a crank. You could say "good morning" and his smart ass would say, "What's good about it?" I would ask him, "What kind of church do you go to with your attitude being so nasty?" He would play it off like it's just my dry sense of humor. I don't mean harm. I'm just playing. I didn't care for it or him, so I avoided him sometimes and would talk to him every now and then. I can remember one conversation I told him he needed some medication because he was crazy. The good that came from meeting Buck was he inspired me to start this project; he said he was researching the different dating sites for a re-search paper for class. The lightbulb went off and piqued my interest because I've met some interesting people from the site and you have to write about some of them because people wouldn't believe it . Some of his research he shared was 65 percent of the women of these sites goes there pure-ly for sex. So his theory concluded my point that in my opinion, the sites are a form of modern-day prostitution.

Chapter 34

Mr. Caden as he called himself was on the line. We talked and exchanged pictures; our conversations were good. He said he was in his field of engineering for over fifteen years, had adult kids, and was just looking for someone to share his world with. As I was driving home one afternoon, he sent me a photo of himself and I kept looking at this picture because he looked familiar to me. I looked closer and realized I met this man and went out with him once over twenty years ago. This blew my wig back! At first I wasn't going to say anything, but I asked him, did he use to drive a navy 5.0 Mustang that had "Get the hoe" on the rear bumper. He confirmed it was him, and we went down memory lane and came to the conclusion it wasn't a bad date; it was just bad timing. My eldest son was a toddler at that time, and I was still with his father, so we only had that one date. We were blown away at our discovery and continued discussing careers, family, and how life has been treating us in the last twenty-five years. I invited him over to a family gathering; he was a no-show and our conversations became less frequent, especially when he sent me picture, and I zoomed in on his face in the mouth area in particular, and it looked like he had herpes on his lip. Thank God he didn't show up spreading his germs and cold sores all over the place. LMAO!

Chapter 35

I met Thomas; he was an electrician. Our first and only date was at Pepe's for drinks. When I saw him, he was a little on the short side for my taste, but he had a nice build. We began talking. I told him I worked in law enforcement. He then told me he needed to be honest and stated, "I just did seven years in the federal joint for selling drugs." I told him I appreciate his honesty, but in my line of work, it would be a conflict of interest, and this was our last meeting. As the conversation continued, he asked what department I worked for. I told him. He then said, "You may know my ex-girlfriend." He told her name and said she just contacted him a month ago to check on him. I told him I know her very well and worked with her for years. We continued casual conversation. We both knew it wasn't going anywhere, which was cool. We ate, and after two blue motherfuckers, it was time to go. Different lifestyles, careers, paths, and strokes. The thing about me, if I met someone and they dated one of my friends, girlfriends, or family members, they are off limits. When I returned to work, I pulled the young lady to the side and told her

I met someone she knew. I gave her the name of the guy, and she didn't recognize it. I then described him and the lightbulb went off. She said that's not his real name. Now I was looking confused and she explained he had issues with people on the streets and that was an alias. Then she went into a thing and asked me if I told him I knew her. I said yes and she said, "He bogus as soon as you told him you knew me. He should have stopped talking to you and got up and left. He was my high school sweetheart." She said, "I can't wait to talk him."

I looked at this girl like she was crazy ass hell; they both been out of high school for over twenty years; that was BANANAS!

Chapter 36

Sherman, the associate pastor, an acclaimed newly gospel recording artist, and a professor. Our initial conversation, he didn't disclose he was a preacher, and I didn't know then, but I know now why he didn't share that information. He was from Merriville and worked in the health field, had two sons, one in college, had two degrees, and he owned his own home and two cars. He was very knowledgeable about world news, our black history, and of course, the Bible. We talked a few more times and decided to meet at a fast food restaurant I was impressed; he was tall, nice, solid build, and smelled good, so I decided to entertain the preacher for a little while. He appeared to be respectful and decent until this buzzard showed me he was the devil in disguise.

The first warning bell was he asked if my pussy was blond or shaved out of the blue. I told him, "You are about to blow it already with your mouth." I reiterated to him I was not interested. "No one-night stands, married men, pimps, users, fuck buddies, and you have replied to my profile because all that is clearly stated in black and white. So with all this said, it's not too late to delete my name from your phone."

He apologized over and over again and promised it would never happen again. His next question was if I believe I am ready for the ministry. He says it comes with a lot of money, power, and prestige. I thought about it in my mind, and I knew I wasn't ready to allow anyone to dictate what I can wear, that I couldn't swear anymore, or the killer, no more cocktails. All, hell naw so I was home one night, sipping some champagne, my drink of choice, getting nice, and he called and asked me to come over for dinner. I accepted the invitation with a second bottle of champagne in tow, ready to enjoy the rest of my night.

Chapter 37

I'm driving, checking out my surroundings; this ain't Merriville, this Gary. I pulled up; it was a nice house, and I can see both his cars, one looking out of commission—that's one strike against him for lying about where he lived. I entered his home and looked around; it was dusty as hell with this old Sanford and Son–looking furniture. He was always bragging about what he has, and from the looks of it, he was a big, fat liar. I gave him my champagne to put in the refrigerator; we proceeded to go his bedroom. It was a full-size bed and a twin-size right next to it. I asked, "Whose twin bed is that?"

He said, "My kid." I didn't want to act like I was better than him so I sat on the edge of the full-size bed. We kissed. He laid down and pulled my pants down, taking my panties off in one swift motion. He began to suck and lick my pussy like it was the last supper. With his tongue skills, it didn't take a sister at all—the bust that first nut. Thinking it was over, he kept going for seconds, tugging and tongue kissing my clit with expertise, and I came again. Damn! With the buzz from the champagne, I was feeling myself. He stood up and wiped his face and laid down like, "My turn."

I'm not selfish like that, and since he did such a good job slurping up my cum and swallowing after my second nut. Fuck it. I looked at his short, stubby, thick dick and went to work. My tongue sliding up and down his shaft and tickling his balls with my fingertips. By his moans, I knew he was enjoying himself. I sucked and slurped on his dick until he came on my hand from jerking his dick slowly up and down as he panted, barely catching his breath after the earth-shattering blowjob.

Chapter 38

I got up and got dressed, went in his bathroom, washed my hands and my pussy, and he continued laying there in his glory, bragging about that wonderful act I just performed. He said, "Where are you going?"

I said, "Home." I said, "No sex, no condoms."

He pleaded for me to stay and said he could run to the store for some condoms. I said, "No, please give me my bottle. I'm ready to go." As he was retrieving my bottle, I was looking at the refrigerator, but he was bending down, getting my bottle out of a mini fridge. I knew it was definitely time to go home. I got my bottle and put up the two fingers deuces just a like a nigger get yours and run. He still texts me daily scriptures and calls, begging for more. I explained to him that was the wrong direction, and I wanted more than a sexual relationship. He told me to keep doing the wonderful things I did with my mouth to him and he would love me forever. The things that would come out of his filthy mouth was unbelievable. As an associate minister, someone who is building his own church, and future gospel singer starting his musical career with some well-established singers in the industry today. I was disappointed in him; he met Trixie that night and he will never forget Hurricane Katrina was there. I bet, if his congregation knew the closet freak he really was, he wouldn't be sending out the scriptures every day. Smh.

Chapter 39

Now, it was Ronnie's turn. Up to bat, he was physically my type, but his mouth was reckless. A single father of one daughter, an engineer, and financially stable. We talked on the phone; our conversations were good, and we exchanged pictures and everything started fine. He asked me to send him a picture of myself in jeans or a dress. I gave him a warning and told him I'm not on the site just for a physical relationship. I'm on here to really meet someone to start a relationship. Not for money, not for looks, but for someone's heart, so if he was just looking for a physical relationship, I was not the one for him. He was pleased with the pictures I sent him, and then he dropped the bomb. He sent me a damn near nude picture with only a towel covering his dick. Again I told him he took this to another level; he laughed and disregarded the words I spoke and continued to send other nude pictures and telling me to come sit on his face.

Don't get me wrong, he had a body and fine, be his

main objective was getting some pussy. The Trixie in me wanted to go fuck the shit out of him, but the lady in me passed, but I was so tempted. He said he wanted me in his life, and he was a good man, and if I wanted that in my life, I better get *him*. Also saying, "Let's get together. Come over and make love to me and start us, and I want to fuck you and make love to you at the same time." wow!

I responded to this buzzard, "You don't know me, and we've never met face-to-face and he was a natural-born fool. He responded, "Shut up, Trina, and just bring that ass over here." It was confirmed. He was a CERTIFIED FOOL!

Chapter 40

That motherfucker just disregarded everything I said, and by blocking him, I hope he got the picture. Another one not taking no for an answer is Barry, a train engineer, with two adult kids, lives alone, has a car, and has beautiful hazel eyes. I know you wonder why he isn't Mr. Right. He's nice and respectful, plus our friendship has been ongoing for over a year now, and we only went out to dinner once. Our issue is timing; our work schedules do not work for us at all. I have a 7-3 shift set schedule. He is on call twenty-four hours, seven days a week. You can't plan a date in advance because you never know when he will be called in. Also, whenever he has had time, he would always ask me to stop by his home after I leave work, not knowing what kind of day I've had working in the hostile and stressful environment I work in. After I leave that crazy-ass place, I don't feel like stopping by nobody's damn house. I'm fighting over an hour of traffic to and from five days out of my week. I may have been more motivated if he would suggest the movies, a concert, or even dinner instead of saying, "Come by my house so we can get to know each other better. Keep the porch light on." Lol. This guy Larone, fifty-three years old, worked at the post office, blew up my profile with messages about how he wanted to meet me, talk to me, or just to get to know me better. So I decided to call him. Our conversation went smooth. Someone I found interesting so I gave him a try. As days passed, we've kept in contact with each other over the phone. Our conversations were brief, but his text appeared that he was a little slow.

Chapter 41

Our date was coming the next week, and we were going to the movies. I kept an open mind and just wanted to see how the turn was going to be. We both pulled up. I was on one side of the parking lot; he was on the other. I called him to let him know I was walking to the front of the theater. I could see him standing at his car, looking lost. I called him again and was wondering why he wasn't picking up the phone. He opens his car door and reaches down and answers the phone, and I tell him, "I'm waiting on you." He approaches; he was handsome, tall, with hazel eyes. In my mind, I'm like, "Yes, he pays." We go in; he asked if I wanted anything. I say no, and we go into the movies. Little to almost no conversation and no physical connection, a DUD. After the movie was over, we said our good-byes, and I sped off; he acted like he was scared or maybe had some warrants. I should have checked his background a little closer. Let me backpedal; how can I forget this clown. Tom from Indianapolis was forty-six years old, had two adult kids, plus the grandfather of one, was tall, handsome, and had the prettiest smile. Our conversation started good; he sent me some handsome pictures of himself and the weirdest things, lady's shoes. I didn't understand, but he had good taste. So we chose to meet up, and he took the two and a half hour drive from Indianapolis to Schereville to meet little old me.

Chapter 42

It was a bitter cold night, and we're both up in identical cars at the Holiday Inn on a Sunday night. We got out, looked at each other, and breathed a sigh of relief and smiled. He was a little on the slim side but was handsome. We entered the room and hugged; he smelled of light cologne and liquor. I asked if he had been drinking while driving; he smirked, and I disregarded the look because he was reeking. That was a turnoff, him smelling like brewery. I was like, fuck it. I came too far to meet him, so I drank a couple of glasses of champagne and loosened up a little. We laid down together on the bed side by side, and I asked him again what he had to drink. He said, "Just a beer."

I knew he was lying because whatever it was, was coming out his pores. The more I drank, the nicer I became, so we kissed. It wasn't so bad now since I had liquor breath too, plus he was a good kisser, but his breath was still awful. I put on my big girl drawers and said, "Fuck it, let's get this over with." I began stroking his dick through his underwear and licking his nipples, and he started moaning and putting baby oil on his dick, and I noticed that this guy at age fifty was not circumcised. I was done. I immediately turned over on my side, still fully clothed, and told him good night because I was going to sleep. I began drifting off and felt his hand rubbing my ass and back, saying to himself, "Damn, I want to fuck." I was playing sleep and got tired of him and finally turned back and said, "Pull your dick out so I can jag you off." He put on his famous oil. I stroked the uncircumcised, deformed-looking dick like liquid gold was coming out. I wanted this shit done quick. He started cumming in no time; it was disgusting he let so much cum. I thought he was going to pass out from dehydration; it was so thick I scrubbed my hand damn near an hour. By now, it was almost daybreak; he went down to car to get his clothes. He was going to visit some relatives in Gary. By the time he made it back to the room, I was suited and booted, fully dressed and ready to go. He said, "Why did you get dressed? I wanted a round 2."

I gave him a "nigger, please" look and threw up the deuces. He still texts to check on me from time to time; that was our first and definitely our last.

Chapter 43

After that, I was at the end of my rope, and giving up on dating—period, then I met Jaden and Joshua, my finale of my online dating journey at the same damn time. I thought. First, Jaden is a father of five, fifty-one years of age, and a director of a nursing facility. He was a very nice guy; we talked and met up at Buffalo Wild Wings for drinks and dinner and was an instant hit. I told him I wanted to go see Eric Roberson, and he surprised me with VIP tickets at the popular winery in downtown area. Plus, he got me a battery for my edger and told me he would paint my house for no charge, and we had been only talking a few weeks. Pinch me, I must be dreaming. He was very attentive; we would talk every day a few times throughout the day to make sure I was okay, and I would do the same; he was the caretaker of his elderly dad—that was his main priority. He called me one day and told me he looked at my Facebook page and recognized a young lady; he asked how close we were. I said we went to high school over thirty years ago, and I had just recently seen her at our reunion. He explained he dated her a couple of years out of high school before she went to the navy, and if she and I were real close, he couldn't date me. I respected him at a new level and was totally in agreement; we continued and went to the concert and had a ball. I was liking Jaden, but his insecurity and trust issue would interfere with our growth; he wanted a relationship, but he wasn't willing to put trust in no one.

Chapter 44

Mr. nigger please, you work at UPS. No, seriously, Joshua father of two, grandfather of one, business owner, and employed in his field over twenty years. We connected and talked and agreed to get a glimpse of each other since we lived in near each other. We met in the supermarket parking. I pulled up; he was there, posted up on his motorcycle with a big-ass grin. We laughed and talked for about an hour as if we know each other way before this day. I was checking him out up and down and noticed this bulge through his jeans lying on his thigh. My mind was like, "Can you imagine how big it is when it gets hard!" We ended our night with a hug, and he smelled good, so I was already looking forward to our future date.

We talked each day, getting to know each more and more and enjoying our newfound friendship. Date night came; he picked me up and we went to the theater and the movie started and so did we. Our first kiss was so passionate and heated it was off the chain; we started touching, caressing, and fondling each other like there was no tomorrow. Our foreplay was so sensual and intense. Our tongues danced and twirled around so much we both felt dizzy. He laid my hand on his rock-hard dick—OMG! I haven't felt a dick that big since my Jersey boo. We took breaks to catch our breath and watch some of the movie. I know the people around us were like, "Go get a room." He turned to me before the movie was over, and he said, "Let's go." Trixie was like, "Hell yeah." Catrina said no. I was sitting there like I had the devil on one shoulder and an angel on the other. We got to up to leave before we exit the theater; he grabbed me and covered my mouth with his and deep tongued me with his thick tongue and his juicy lips like he sealed for the night. We got in the car and continued talking about the effect we had on each other, coming to the conclusion that life was short, nothing or no one is promised, and let's enjoy our moment.

Chapter 45

We tiptoed in (his children was home), we made it to the bedroom, he laid me on my back, and he spread my legs open in a "V" and slid my panties to the side and began to lick and taste my nectar of my juicy pussy. Evidently, he couldn't suck like he wanted it, so he took my panties off and devoured my pussy like he was on death row, like it was his last meal. I damn near let out a tsunami in his mouth in 2.2 seconds. We kissed more and more; our intimacy level was so high we didn't need penetration. The pattern of our breathing, the sweet taste of my pussy on his lips, and his touch, I was almost ready to cum again, anticipating his thickness splitting me open. He told me this night was mine, sit back and enjoy his dick ride. His dick felt so good it hurt, but I took it all in like a champ. He was so arrogant, I couldn't let him win. I fucked the shit out of him to the point he looked down at me and said, "You are fucking me." We both came together; it was explosive. We slept the rest of the night away, both with smiles and satisfaction written all over our faces. We carried on months later, seeing each other when time permitted. Our friendship was like a tug-of-war. We both had our own, so we didn't need each other financially. We were independent and bullheaded with the boss mentality. I can and will not tolerate disrespect, and his way of playing is the way I act when I have had too much to drink. The writing on the wall was, I would fuck around and lose my job if I continue to deal with this man. I was really liking him and wanted to see how our future would play out but it seemed the closer he got to me, he would flip the script and push me away. I threw in the white towel. Joshua, for the record, you won.

Chapter 46

A man reached out to me on the site, claiming he was a renowned author of various novels and a radio blog talk show host. He stated how he would love to get to know the beautiful person on the pictures and left me his credentials, his phone numbers, his e-mail addresses, and advised me to Google him to learn more about him. I Googled him, and sure enough, this author existed and had different pictures of himself, his list of books, and his radio guest and topics. We talked on the phone, and he was overjoyed. I reached out to him. Physically, he was not my type, but his personality was so energetic and positive, I knew if nothing romantically became of us, we could be good friends. After three weeks of talking on the phone, I thought it was strange he wasn't in a rush to meet in person and was content with talking on the phone two or three times of day. My lightbulb lit up; when we began exchanging pictures, the pictures he sent me were the exact pictures on Google and Facebook. Hmmmmmmmmmmm, so I started digging but keeping it cool to see what this man's intention were. He never asked me about my family, job, or where I lived—just general conversations, so I didn't feel it was a money scam. I listened to his radio show so the voices matched. Every conversation he would brag on how great of an author he was and how he was going to be a millionaire in a couple of years and how much he wanted a relationship and future together. He said he was completing his eleventh book and even sent me a copy of a draft of the book and asked what I thought about his work. Then I looked at his Facebook page closer and checked the photos, how many friends he had, or even responses. He had no friends and the photos were the same as one on Google nothing different. I was like, who is this person and I am being catfished. He asked me several times to purchase one of books because he knew I would enjoy it, and he really wanted me to read it.

Chapter 47

I didn't feel secure about sharing my credit card information on his personal so-called publication page. I decided I was going to call his bluff after four weeks talking on the phone. I said "Send me a different picture, a selfie, or let's meet in person."

He went ballistic. He said, "You are selfish and only think of yourself and you are not the one for me."

I said all this because I want to see the person behind the voice. Wow. He broke down and sent me a picture of a Polaroid picture of him posted on a bulletin board. Now I'm really puzzled, wondering why this man does not want to me to see him face-to-face or his true physical identity.

A day later, he texted and said, "Let's meet this week. Give me your address so I can pick you up because I'm a gentleman."

I told him no. I would meet him in a public place. Of course, I never heard from him again. I pray that whoever this person is, he is not using the online dating platform or in other method to meet women and to cause any harm. Till this day, I still wonder who the mystery man behind the computer is.

Be safe, ladies.